The LITTLE FISH

That Got Away

story by Bernadine Cook • pictures by Crockett Johnson

HarperCollins*Publishers*

The Little Fish That Got Away   Text copyright © 1956, 1984 by Bernadine Cook   Illustrations copyright © 1956 by Crockett Johnson   New color palette copyright © 2005 by the Estate of Ruth Krauss   Printed in the U.S.A. All rights reserved.
Library of Congress Catalog Card no. 56005419   ISBN 0-06-055713-3 — ISBN 0-06-055714-1 (lib. bdg.)
Typography by Drew Willis   1 2 3 4 5 6 7 8 9 10   ❖   First HarperCollins Edition.
Originally published in hardcover by Addison Wesley Publishing Company in 1956.

Once upon a time
there was a little boy
who liked to go fishing.

See,
there he goes,
over there on the other page.

He went fishing every day.

But he never,
no never,
caught any fish.

In fact,
all he ever did catch
was a bad cold.

Except ONE day,
and you will never,
no never,
believe it —

He dug some worms
   and he put them in a can.
He got the long tree limb
   that he called a fish pole.

He put the pole over his shoulder.

And off he went.

He came to his favorite spot
where he never caught
any fish.
He put a worm on the pin,
and the pin in the water,
and he waited—

And waited,
and waited.

Then he saw
    a **GREAT GREAT** big fish.
It swam around, and around,
    and around, and around,
    and around and around
    and around.

Like this.

It looked at the worm on the pin.
It wiggled its tail.
Then it swam
around, and around,
and around and around
and around—

Right back to wherever
it came from.
Just like this.
Yes, it did.

The little boy
waited
and waited—

And waited.

Then along came
a **GREAT** big fish.
And it swam around,
and around, and
around and around
and around.

Just like this.

It looked at the worm on the pin.
It waggled its tail.
Then it swam
    around, and around,
    and around and around
    and around—

Right back to wherever
    it came from.
Just like this.
                    Yes, it did.

The little boy
waited
and waited—

And waited.

Then along came
a BIG fish.
And it swam around,
and around, and
around and around
and around.

Like this.

It looked at the worm on the pin.
It wiggled its tail.
Then it swam
  around, and around,
  and around and around
  and around—

Right back to wherever
  it came from.
Just like this.
            Yes, it did.

So,
   the little boy
   waited
   and waited—

And waited.

Then along came
a **LITTLE** fish.
And it swam around,
and around, and
around and around
and around.

Just like this.
Yes, it did.

It looked at the worm on the pin.
It waggled its tail.
Then it swam
 around, and around,
 and around and around
 and around—

Right back to wherever
 it came from.
Just like this.
      Yes, it did.

The poor little boy thought sadly
that he wasn't going to catch
any fish again that day.
But he looked down—

In the water.

And there in the water was
the **GREAT GREAT** big fish
coming back again.
It swam around, and around,
and around and around
and around.

It looked at the worm
on the pin.
It waggled its tail.
Then—

It ate the worm.
And the little boy pulled
the GREAT GREAT big fish
out of the water—

And put him in the basket
he kept under the tree,
in case he should ever
catch any fish.

He put another worm on the pin,
put the pin in the water,
and pretty soon,
the GREAT big fish
came back again.
It swam around, and around.

It looked at the worm
on the pin.
It waggled its tail.
Then—

It ate the worm.
And the little boy pulled
the GREAT big fish
out of the water—

And put him in the basket
he kept under the tree,
in case he should ever
catch any fish.

He put another worm on the pin,
put the pin in the water,
and pretty soon,
the BIG fish
came back again.
It swam around, and around.

It looked at the worm
on the pin.
It waggled its tail.
Then —

It ate the worm.
And the little boy pulled
the BIG fish
out of the water —

And put him in the basket
he kept under the tree,
in case he should ever
catch any fish.

He put another worm on the pin,
put the pin in the water,
and waited
and waited—

And waited.

And, pretty soon, the LITTLE fish
came back again.
It swam around, and around,
and around and around
and around.
Like this.

It looked at the worm
on the pin.
It waggled its little tail.
It sniffed at the worm.

The little boy sat very quiet
and thought —

Hurry up, little fish,
and eat the worm.
Then I will go home
and show Mother and Father
all the fish I caught.

But —

The little fish didn't bite the worm.
It looked, and looked.
And then,
    it swam around, and around,
    and around and around and
    around—

Right back
    to wherever it
    came from.

And the little boy
LAUGHED,
right out loud.

Yes, he did.

Then he picked up his basket with
the **GREAT GREAT** big fish in it,
and the **GREAT** big fish in it,
and the **BIG** fish in it.

And he started home.
Like this.

When he got home,
   he showed his mother
   the fish.
And she was very happy
   to have the fish.
She cleaned them,
   and cooked them
   for supper that night.

His Father ate the GREAT big fish.
His Mother ate the BIG fish.
And the little boy ate
the GREAT GREAT big fish,
because he was so hungry.
Yes, he did.

While they were eating,
the little boy told
how he caught the fish,
and how the little fish
wouldn't eat the worm
on the pin.
And they all laughed and laughed
about the LITTLE fish

that

got

away.